SEQUENCING SEAL

WRITTEN BY BETTY ISAAK
ILLUSTRATED BY BEV ARMSTRONG

Contents

Copyright © 1982
THE LEARNING WORKS, INC.
Santa Barbara, CA 93111
All rights reserved.
Printed in the United States of America.

Introduction

Carmen Montemayor
PO Box 3283
East Chicago IN 46312-8283

Sequencing Seal has been written to help you assist your child increase his or her understanding of logical order and skill in arranging things in proper sequence. It is divided into two main sections. The first section contains brief descriptions of simple games and activities you and your child can enjoy together using common materials you probably have around the house.

The second section contains activity sheets for your child. On each sheet are simple instructions you can read to your child. In the upper left-hand corner is the name of a familiar process, such as digging a hole, getting dressed, or taking a bath. On the page are pictures of different stages of various activities. The child is asked to indicate the correct order for these picture sequences. These activities will involve your child in a variety of valuable educational experiences, including

- naming and describing
- comparing and ordering
- drawing and coloring
- cutting and pasting
- assembling and building
- combining and cooking

Sequencing is the process of arranging thoughts, objects, and events in logical order. Sequencing allows us to accomplish tasks by following a prescribed series of steps and to connect present with past and future. It helps children see how today's events are the result of yesterday's occurrences. It is an important skill for beginning readers because, to read, they must be able to recognize subtle differences in letter order and to realize the importance of these differences. To write words, they must reproduce the letters in proper order. To write stories, they must understand the importance of a beginning, a middle, and an ending.

In doing these activities with your child, first have him or her look at the pictures. Second, discuss the sequence, or process, that is being pictured and point out how the pictures are related. Third, read and explain the activity instructions to your child and have him or her color, mark, or paste as directed to indicate the correct order for two of the pictures. If he or she hesitates, ask a prompting question such as, *Which came first?* or, *What happened first? What happened next? What happened last?* Fourth, when you are certain that your child knows what order is being asked for and how to indicate that order, allow him or her to continue in the same manner until the activity has been completed.

Sequencing is an important skill. It enables us to think logically, to see the relationships between cause and effect and between actions and consequences, and to understand how our input can affect the outcome. It can be improved with practice. This book is designed to help you give your child that all-important practice.

Sequencing Games and Activities

In the Kitchen

Dinner Winner

Have your child help you prepare a simple meal. Before you begin, make a chart showing the order of preparation so that each dish will be ready on time.

1. Make the pudding and put it in the refrigerator to cool.
2. Start cooking the spaghetti.
3. Butter the bread and put it in the oven.
4. Make the salad.
5. Finish making the spaghetti.

Pixie Pizzas

English muffins	weiners
pizza flavored catsup	pitted olives
grated cheese	

Slice weiners ¼" thick. Cut up olives. Spread muffin halves with catsup. Add cheese, weiner slices, and olives as desired. Heat under broiler until cheese melts.

Recipe Reasoning

Select a simple recipe and set out all of the ingredients. Then read the instructions to your child and have him or her help you make the dish described. Give hints for any forgotten steps. As you enjoy eating what you have made, talk about the importance of following a recipe in order.

Sweet Story

Help your child bake and decorate a cake for some special occasion. As you work together, talk about the steps in order (for example, greasing pans, mixing ingredients, pouring batter into pans, baking, cooling, mixing icing, frosting layers, and decorating the top and sides.

Dish Delight

Name the steps involved in dishwashing (for example, clearing the table, scraping the plates, washing, rinsing, drying, and putting the dishes away), and talk about the order in which these steps are usually done. Using magazine pictures, help your child make a chart showing the steps in order. Then have your child help with this task.

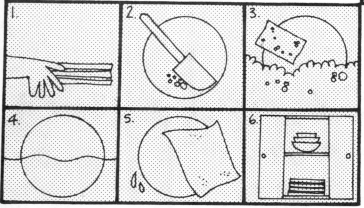

Sequencing Games and Activities

In the Bedroom

Tale Tellers

Read a favorite book together. Then have your child name or describe the main events in order.

Fairy Tale Facts

Tell a familiar fairy tale, leaving out one important event. Then ask your child what part of the story was missing and when it should have happened.

Outfit Order

Using catalog or magazine pictures, make a chart to help your child learn how to get dressed. On the chart show a child in the various stages of dressing. Talk with your child about the importance of putting on underwear *before* outer wear and following the correct order.

Sunrise Sequence

Using catalog or magazine pictures, help your child make a chart showing his or her morning routine. Go over the order of the steps with your child (for example, get out of bed, wash face, get dressed, brush hair, make bed, eat breakfast, put dishes by sink, and brush teeth).

In the Bathroom

Sea Stories

When it is bath time, have your child select some favorite tub toys. Ask your child to make up and tell you a simple story about these toys while playing with them in the tub.

Doll Wash

Talk about the steps involved in taking a bath. Have your child go through these steps with a washable doll (for example, undress, wash, dry, and dress).

Sequencing Seal
© 1982—The Learning Works, Inc.

Sequencing Games and Activities

In the Garage, Workshop, or Laundry Room

Wood Works

Talk about where wood comes from and the steps it follows to get to you. Then plan a simple wood project with your child. Talk about the steps you will follow to complete the project. Cut, sand, glue, nail, and paint to complete the project you have planned.

Laundry Line-up

Have your child help with the laundry. Start by collecting dirty clothes, and continue with sorting, washing, drying, folding, and distributing the clothes to family members.

Outdoors

Plant Pictures

Start a garden with your child. Plant the seeds. Then water, weed, observe growth, and harvest. Help your child make a picture book showing each thing you did in order.

Travel Trails

When driving in your neighborhood, play a game to see if your child can remember the buildings and landmarks in order (for example: a gas station on the corner, a market as you turn the corner, a paint store next to the market).

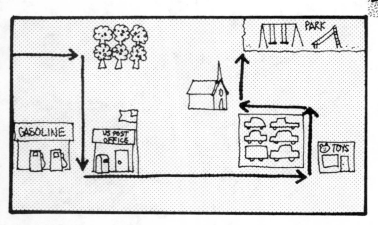

Sequencing Games and Activities

Here, There, and Anywhere

Super Schedule—a.m.

In the morning talk about that day's plans with your child. Use the words *before* and *after* when ordering the day's schedule. Make a chart to show activities in order. Discuss how some things need to be done in sequence while others do not.

Super Schedule—p.m.

As you are having some quiet time together before your child goes to sleep, talk over the day's events. Discuss the order in which things were done, and how this order may have differed from the chart you made.

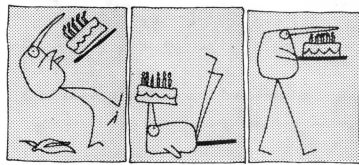

Memories and Make-Believe

Have a family storytelling time. Ask one family member to start a story and another member to add to it. Have members continue creating the story in turn until it is finished. In addition to stories, personal experiences, such as a vacation, could be recalled.

Silly Sequences

Cut out several cartoon strips that do not use words. Cut the pictures in one strip apart and put them in an envelope. Do the same for each of the other strips. Have your child select one envelope, take out the pictures, and arrange them in the correct sequence.

Get a Letter

Write a letter for your child to a special relative or friend. Have your child tell you in order the interesting things that have happened recently so that you can write them down. Mail the letter. Receiving a letter in return will make this an exciting exercise.

Program Perception

Watch a television show with your child. During each commercial, cover the screen with a towel, turn the volume down, and ask your child what he or she thinks will happen next.

quencing Seal
1982—The Learning Works, Inc.

Watch the Birdie

Mark these pictures to show how a bird builds its nest. Color one leaf in the first picture of the sequence, color two leaves in the second picture, and so on.

Chicken's Delight

Arrange these pictures to show what happens when an egg hatches. Draw a line from the first picture in this sequence to the second picture. Then continue to connect the pictures in order.

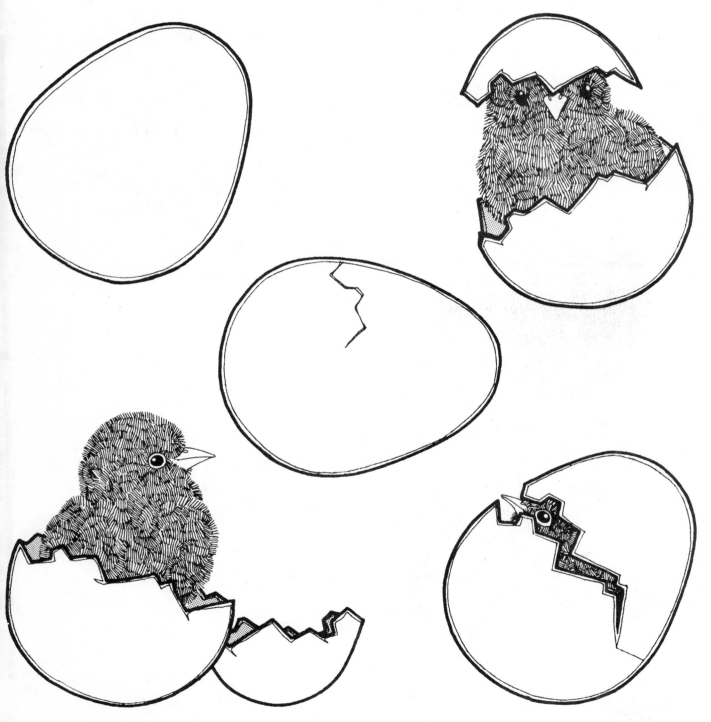

From Seed to Weed

Mark these pictures to show what happens as a plant grows. Draw a line from the seed to the picture that shows the next step in growth. Continue to draw lines connecting the pictures in order.

Picture Perfect

Mark these pictures to show how people grow up. Color one corner on the first picture in this sequence, color two corners on the second picture, and so on.

Doggie Dig

Mark these pictures to show what happens as a dog digs a hole. Draw one dot on the dog in the first picture of this sequence, draw two dots on the dog in the second picture, and so on.

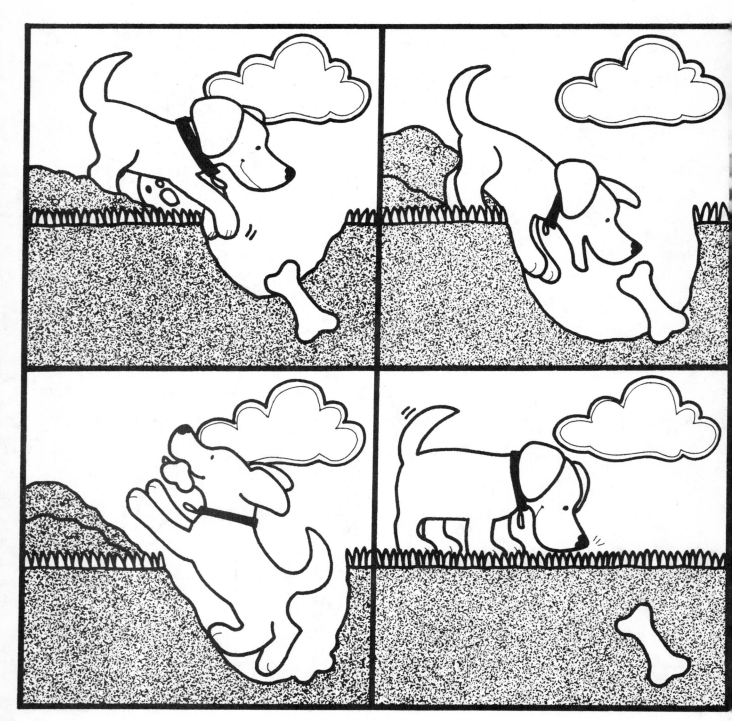

Rub-a-Dub-Dub

Arrange these pictures to show what happens when you take a bath. Draw a line from the first picture in this sequence to the second picture. Then continue to connect the pictures in order.

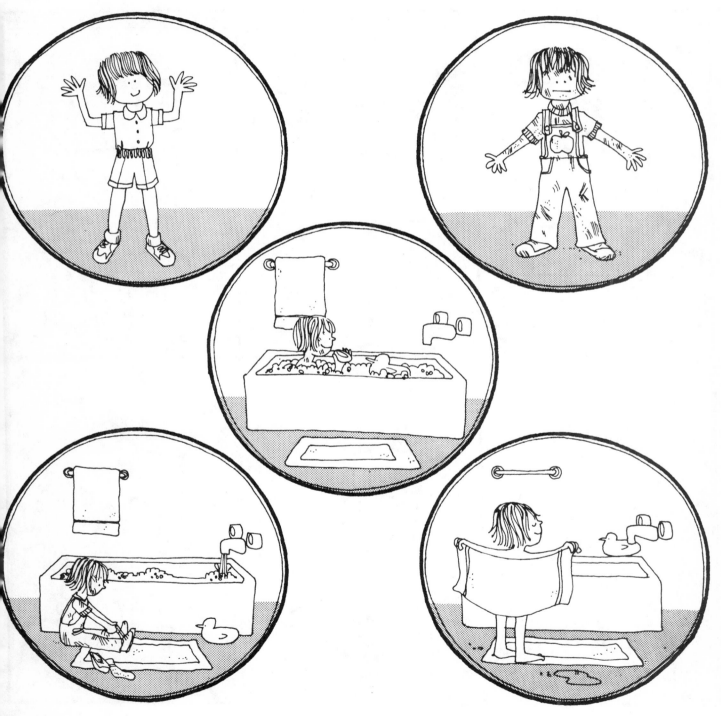

Draw a Dog

Mark these pictures to show how to draw a dog. Color one crayon in the first picture of the sequence, color two crayons in the second picture, and so on.

One, Two, Buckle My Shoe

Mark these pictures to show what happens when you get dressed. Color one square on the first picture in this sequence, color two squares on the second picture, and so on.

Building Blocks

Mark these pictures to show what happens when you build with blocks. Color one square in the first picture of this sequence, color two squares in the second picture, and so on.

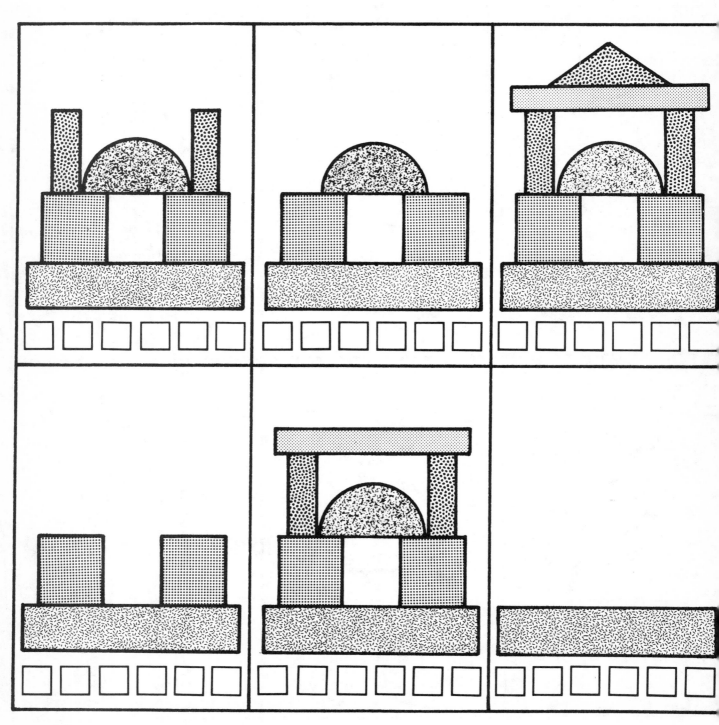

How Does Your Garden Grow?

Mark these pictures to show how a garden grows. Color one square in the first picture of this sequence, color two squares in the second picture, and so on.

Pat-a-Cake

Mark these pictures to show what happens when a cake is baked. Color one square in the first picture of this sequence, color two squares in the second picture, and so on.

Something's Fishy

Number these pictures to show what happens when someone goes fishing. Cut out the numbered tails at the bottom of this page. Paste them on the fish to indicate the correct order.

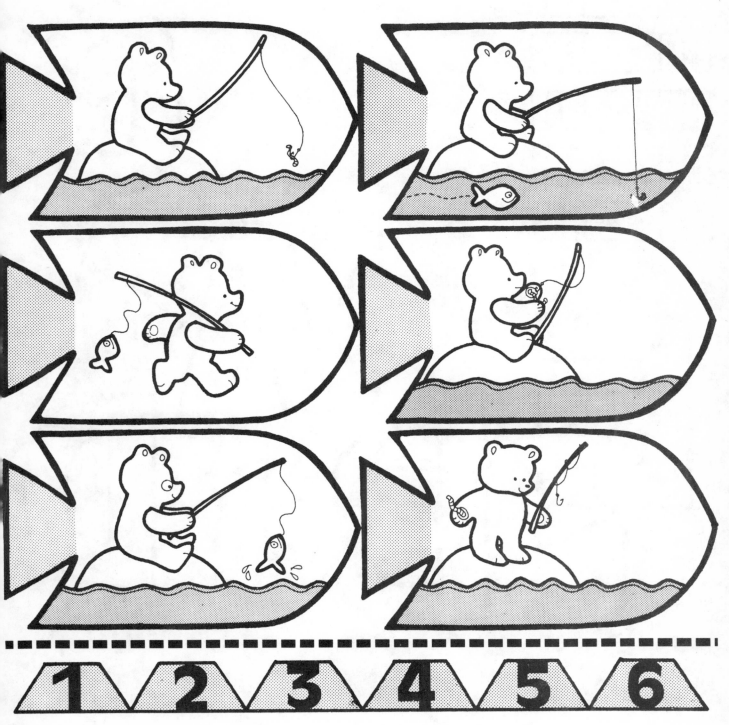

Letter Parade

Color the crayons as marked. Then color the first letter of the alphabet red, color the second letter blue, and so on.

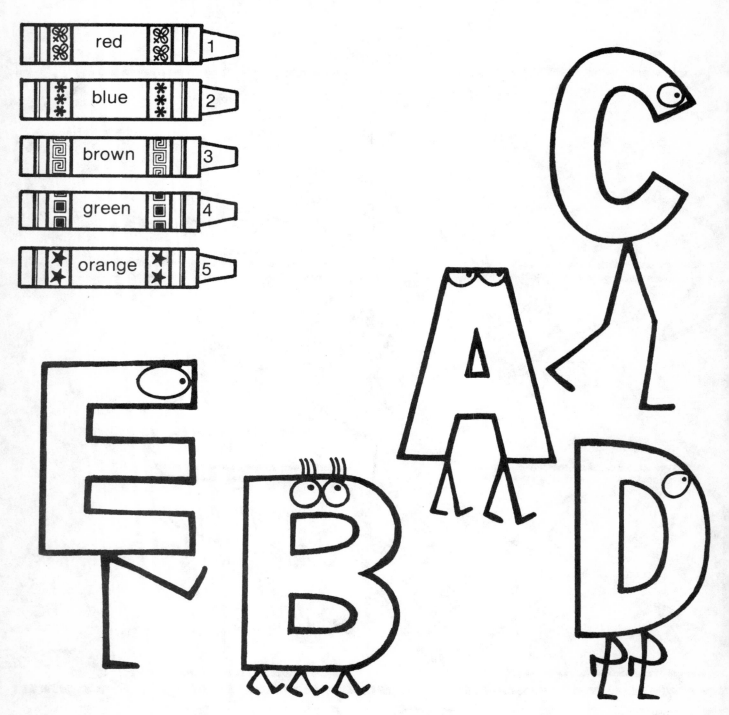

Silly Snowman

Number these pictures to show what happens when someone builds a snowman. Cut out the numbered snowballs at the bottom of the page. Paste them on the snowmen to indicate the correct order.

Sequencing Seal
© 1982—The Learning Works, Inc.

Number Roundup

Count from 1 to 6. Then fill in the blanks below with the correct number from the lasso.

This Award
is given to

_____
(name of child)

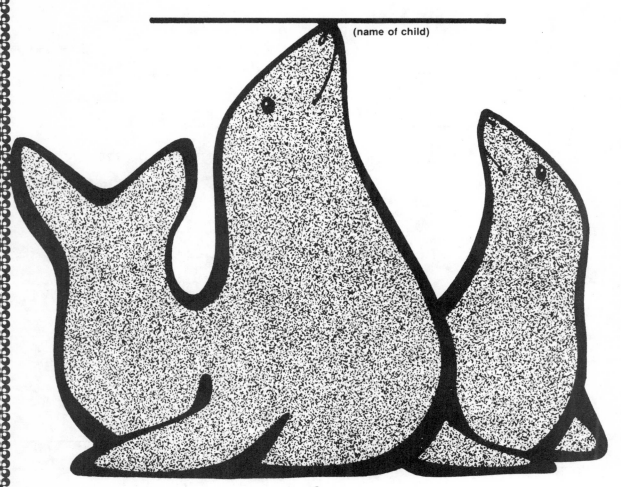

for
simply sensational
Sequencing

_____   _____
(signature of parent)   (date)

NOTES